CAMILA
THE BAKING STAR

written by ALICIA SALAZAR

illustrated by THAIS DAMIÃO

PICTURE WINDOW BOOKS

a capstone imprint

Camila the Star is published by Picture Window Books,
an imprint of Capstone.
1710 Roe Crest Drive
North Mankato, Minnesota 56003
www.capstonepub.com

Library of Congress Cataloging-in-Publication Data
Names: Salazar, Alicia, 1973– author. | Damião, Thais, illustrator.
Title: Camila the baking star / by Alicia Salazar; illustrated by Thais Damião.
Description: North Mankato, Minnesota : Picture Window Books, a Capstone
imprint, [2021] | Series: Camila the star | Audience: Ages 5–7. | Audience: Grades
K–1. | Summary: Camila and her Papá enter a televised baking competition, but
trying to do everything herself results in a mess so Papá helps to bake cake pops
that could make them stars.
Identifiers: LCCN 2020034905 (print) | LCCN 2020034906 (ebook) | ISBN
9781515882091 (hardcover) | ISBN 9781515883180 (paperback) | ISBN
9781515891819 (pdf)
Subjects: CYAC: Family life—Fiction. | Baking—Fiction. | Contests—Fiction. |
Ability—Fiction. | Hispanic Americans—Fiction.
Classification: LCC PZ7.1.S2483 Caf 2021 (print) | LCC PZ7.1.S2483 (ebook) | DDC
[E]—dc23
LC record available at https://lccn.loc.gov/2020034905
LC ebook record available at https://lccn.loc.gov/2020034906

Designer: Kay Fraser

Printed and bound in the USA. PO 3837

TABLE OF CONTENTS

Meet Camila and Her Family

Papá

Mamá

Ana, age 14

Andres, age 10

Camila, age 7

Spanish Glossary

buena suerte (BWEH-nah SWEHR-teh)—good luck

hojarascas (oh-hah-RAHS-kahs)—Mexican shortbread cookies

leche (LEH-cheh)—milk

Mamá (mah-MAH)—Mom

masa (MAH-sah)—mixture or dough

pan blanco (pahn BLAHN-koh)—white bread

panaderia (pah-nah-deh-REE-ah)—bakery

Papá (pah-PAH)—Dad

Chapter 1

THE CHALLENGE

"We are all out of **pan blanco**," said Mamá.

"I can swing by the **panaderia**," said Papá.

Camila looked up from watching *World Baking Challenge*.

"I want to go too," she said.

Mrs. Ortiz, the owner of the bakery, greeted Camila with a hug. "I have a surprise for you."

She handed Camila a flyer. *World Baking Challenge* was having a parent-child competition.

Camila's eyes sparkled. "Papá, we would be worldwide stars!" she said. "Will you please do it with me? Please?"

"Sure! I baked **hojarascas** for the holidays," he said. "How hard could it be?"

Two weeks after they signed up for the show, Papá got a call. It was Stella, the presenter of the baking show. Camila craned her neck to hear Stella's words.

"You and your daughter are invited to join us for the next competition!" Stella said.

"Yippeee!" Camila clapped her hands.

"We have to practice!" she told Papá. "I really want to go to Paris!"

"What do you want to bake?" asked Papá.

"Cupcakes!" said Camila. "Everyone likes cupcakes."

They set the timer for one hour. They mixed and iced and iced and mixed. They practiced every day.

They practiced so much that the whole family and all of their neighbors got to taste.

They practiced until everyone agreed they had the perfect cupcake.

Chapter 2

LIGHTS, CAMERA, ACTION

Camila leaped out of bed the morning of the competition.

"Can I do this?" Camila wondered. She wrung her hands. "Can I be a star today?"

At the studio, each of the three teams were given aprons.

Stella showed them a kitchen with no walls surrounded by cameras. "This is your station," she said.

Camila and Papá wished
each other **buena suerte**. They
shared a high five.

"Lights, camera, action!" said
the director while clacking the
clapperboard.

"Your challenge today is to make strawberry-iced cake pops. You have 45 minutes," Stella said. "Go!"

"We need to work fast,"
Camila said as she raced around
their kitchen. "If we run out of
time, we will be disqualified!"

"What can I do?" asked
Papá. He reached for the eggs.

"I'll get the eggs and the
leche!" said Camila.

"Do you need some help?" asked Papá. He reached for the bowl.

"No, I can mix it myself!" cried Camila.

"I can help," said Papá.

"I've got this!" said Camila.

Chapter 3

TEAMWORK

Camila mixed the ingredients in a hurry. "I'll be a star!" she thought.

But her mixture was a gloopy, thick mess.

"I can't make cake pops with this!" Camila said with a frown. "I'll never get to Paris!"

She turned to watch the other two teams. They were all working steadily. They were all working *with* their partners.

"Papá, you and I are a team," she said. "I don't have to do everything. We should work together."

"I would be happy to help," said Papá. He adjusted his apron and winked at Camila.

Camila threw the goopy stuff in the trash.

"I'll work on the **masa**," Papá said.

"I'll work on the icing," Camila said.

She stirred. He blended. He dunked. She added the big finish.

They finished the cake pops with one minute to spare.

The judges took a bite of each team's creation. Camila crossed her fingers and gritted her teeth.

"The first-place team is . . .
Camila Maria Flores Ortiz and
her stepdad, Daniel!" Stella said.
"You are going to Paris!"

When they got home from Paris, Mrs. Ortiz asked Camila to make their famous cake pops for the **panaderia**.

"You are a star, Camila!" she said.

"*We* are stars," said Camila. "Papá and I are a perfect team!"

Bake Hojarascas

Camila learned that baking as a team can be fun. Ask a grown-up to be your teammate and bake up a batch of hojarascas. The word *hojarascas* is Spanish for "dry leaves." When you walk on dry leaves, they make a crunching noise. Just like stepping on dried leaves, these cookies will crunch when you bite them!

INGREDIENTS
DOUGH
- ⅔ cup plus 1 tablespoon shortening
- ½ cup sugar
- 2 teaspoons ground cinnamon
- pinch of salt
- 2 cups flour

COATING
- ¼ cup sugar
- 1-1 ½ teaspoon of ground cinnamon

WHAT YOU DO

1. Using a mixer, beat the shortening until light and fluffy in a large bowl.

2. Add the sugar, cinnamon, and salt. Mix until well blended.

3. Gently stir in ½ cup flour and mix. Repeat three times. Stir until all of the flour is well mixed.

4. Cover with plastic and refrigerate for at least 20 minutes.

5. Preheat oven to 325°F. Line two baking sheets with parchment paper.

6. Using a rolling pin, roll out the dough until it is ⅓ inch thick. Cut out cookies with a cookie cutter. Transfer cookies to a baking sheet about 1 inch apart.

7. Bake until the edges turn light gold, about 20 minutes. Let cookies cool on the baking sheet before moving or they will crumble.

8. Mix the sugar and cinnamon coating in a small bowl. Dust the cooled cookies with the mixture.

Glossary

competition (kahm-puh-TIH-shuhn)—a contest between two or more teams or people

disqualified (dis-KWAL-uh-fyed)—stopped from taking part in or winning an activity

presenter (pri-ZEN-ter)—in a show, the person who explains what is going on and introduces guests

station (STAY-shuhn)—an area where someone is assigned to work

studio (STOO-dee-oh)—a place where television shows are made

Think About the Story

1. When the baking competition started, Camila did not want any help at first. Why do you think that is?

2. Would you want to compete in a baking competition? Why or why not?

3. Compare how things went for Camila when she tried to do everything herself to when her papá helped.

4. Make a poster for Mrs. Ortiz's bakery, advertising Camila's cake pops. Be sure to describe their taste!

About the Author

Alicia Salazar is a Mexican American children's book author who has written for blogs, magazines, and educational publishers. She was also once an elementary school teacher and a marine biologist. She currently lives in the suburbs of Houston, Texas, but is a city girl at heart. When Alicia is not dreaming up new adventures to experience, she is turning her adventures into stories for kids.

About the Illustrator

Thais Damião is a Brazilian illustrator and graphic designer. Born and raised in a small city in Rio de Janeiro, Brazil, she spent her childhood playing with her brother and cousins and drawing all the time. Her illustrations are dedicated to children and inspired by nature and friendship. Thais currently lives in California.